Hey Jack! Books

First American Edition 2014
Kane Miller, A Division of EDC Publishing

Text copyright © 2013 Sally Rippin
Illustration copyright © 2013 Stephanie Spartels
Logo and design copyright © 2013 Hardie Grant Egmont

First published in Australia in 2013 by Hardie Grant Egmont

For information contact:
Kane Miller, A Division of EDC Publishing
P.O. Box 470663
Tulsa, OK 74147-0663
www.kanemiller.com
www.edcpub.com
www.usbornebooksandmore.com

Library of Congress Control Number: 2013944868

Printed and bound in the United States of America
12 13 14 15 16 17 18 19
ISBN: 978-1-61067-260-3

Hey Jack!

The Playground Problem

By Sally Rippin

Illustrated by Stephanie Spartels

Kane Miller
A DIVISION OF EDC PUBLISHING

feels like
being quiet

Hands in
pockets

Lonely Mood

Chapter One

This is Jack. Today Jack
is in a lonely mood.
Billie is home sick from
school and Jack has
nobody to play with.

Jack has other friends, but Billie is his **bestest** best friend. The school day feels long and boring without Billie.

At recess, Jack sits under the pepper tree. He draws squiggles in the dust with a stick.

Jack looks up and sees Alex standing in front of him. Alex is in Jack's class. He just got new glasses.

"Hey, Alex," says Jack.
"Nice glasses."

"Thanks," Alex says.
"Hey, do you want to
see something **cool**?"

Jack grins. "OK," he says.
He follows Alex to the far
end of the playground.

Alex points to a mound
of dirt. Jack kneels down.

4

"It's an ants' nest," Alex

whispers. "Those are the

worker ants. They are

carrying food for the

queen ant and her babies."

"Cool," says Jack. He lies on his stomach to see the ants better.

They are so busy! They run in and out of the nest without stopping. Alex lies next to him. Together they watch the ants without talking.

6

Soon the bell rings.

Jack can't believe how

quickly time has passed!

"Shall we come back at lunchtime?" Alex asks.

"Sure!" says Jack happily. They stand up and run back to class.

At lunchtime, Jack and
Alex take some crumbs
from their sandwiches
to the ants' nest.

Jack crouches next to
Alex. He watches the
ants lift the crumbs onto
their backs. The crumbs
look **huge** compared to
the tiny ants.

When the bell rings, Jack stands up and stretches.

"Tomorrow I'll bring some sugar water," says Alex. "They will **love** that. Meet you here at recess?"

"Um…" Jack says.

"Well, Billie might be back at school tomorrow. I'll have to wait to see what she wants to do."

"Oh. OK," says Alex. He looks disappointed.

Jack feels bad. He likes Alex. But Billie is his bestest best friend!

Chapter Two

The next day Billie
is at school. Jack is
happy to see her.
They sit next to each
other in class.

When the bell goes for
recess, Alex walks over.

"Hey, Jack," he says.
"Do you want to
come see the ants?
I've brought some sugar
water. And look!
My brother lent me his
magnifying glass so we
can see them up close."

Jack looks at Billie.

"Do you want to come, Billie?" he says.

Billie **scrunches** up her nose. "Why would I want to look at a bunch of ants?" she says. "No, thanks. I'm playing soccer." She runs outside to join their friends on the field.

Jack looks at Alex.

"Well?" Alex says,
hopefully.

Jack feels his tummy tighten into a knot.

He doesn't know what to do. He really wants to go and see the ants with Alex. But he wants to play with Billie, too.

He takes a deep breath. "Um, maybe another time?" he says.

"OK," mumbles Alex.

Alex hangs his head
and walks out of the
classroom. Jack watches
him go. Then he goes
out to the field to
join Billie.

Jack tries to enjoy the soccer game. But he can't stop thinking about Alex.

He can see Alex sitting by himself on the other side of the playground where the ants' nest is. Jack feels **sorry** for him.

Suddenly, Jack has an idea. "I have to go to the bathroom!" he calls to Billie.

"OK," says Billie. "Hurry back. We're losing!"

Jack runs toward the bathroom. Then, when he thinks Billie isn't watching, he **scoots** around to the ants' nest.

Alex looks very happy
to see him.

"Hey, Jack!" he says.
"Look at the ants! They
love the sugar water."

Jack squats down next
to Alex. He looks
through the magnifying
glass as the ants gather
around the drops of
sugar water. Today
there are more ants
than ever!

Just then the bell rings.
Jack jumps up in a panic.

He can't believe that
recess is over.

Oh no, he thinks. *I must
have been away for ages.
Billie is going to be so
cross with me!*

Chapter Three

Jack runs back to class.
He sits down next to
Billie. She looks at
him and **frowns**.

27

"Where were you?"
she says. "We lost because
of you!"

"Um, I told you. I was in
the bathroom," Jack says.

"No, you weren't," she says crossly. "I saw you with Alex! Why don't you go and sit with *him* if he's your new best friend?"

"He's not!" says Jack quickly. "You're my best friend! I don't even like Alex!"

This isn't really true.

But Jack is so **worried** about Billie being mad, the lie just slips out.

Jack hears someone behind him. He spins around.

Oh no – it's Alex!

He looks very upset.

"Well, I don't like you

either, Jack!" he shouts.

Alex stomps off to

another desk.

Jack feels **sick**. He has lied to the two people he likes most. Now neither of them will want to be his friend!

Ms. Walton comes into the classroom. She starts reading the class a book about dragons.

While he listens to the story, Jack thinks about what he has to do.

When the bell rings for lunch, Jack runs up to Alex and takes a deep breath.

"I'm sorry," he says.
"I didn't mean what I
said before. I like you
a lot! It's just that our
team will lose again if
I don't play soccer at
lunchtime."

"That's okay," Alex
mumbles. "I understand.
I like soccer, too."

"Really?" says Jack,
surprised. "I didn't
know that."

"You never asked," says Alex, shrugging.

Jack **grins**. He has an idea. "Would you play with me and Billie today? We need another player on our team!"

"Really?" says Alex. "Sure!"

"Great!" says Jack.

He puts his arm around

Alex's shoulder.

"Then maybe we can go see the ants together tomorrow?" says Jack. "I don't have to play soccer every day."

Alex grins. "It's a deal!" he says.

They run over to the soccer field.

The game is just about

to start. "Alex is on our

team!" Jack calls out

to Billie.

"Great!" says Billie.

"Now we might win,

finally!"

Jack watches Alex run

around the soccer field.

He is fast and good at
kicking goals. Jack is
surprised.

Alex kicks another goal.
Billie **cheers**, then
looks at Jack and grins.
Jack smiles back. He is
glad she isn't cross with
him anymore.

Billie is his **bestest** best friend. That will never change.

But it's good to have other friends too, he thinks happily. Two friends mean twice the fun!